Itty ♥ Bitty PRINCESS Kitty

12

Mystery at Mermaid Cove

by Melody Mews   illustrated by Ellen Stubbings

LITTLE SIMON

New York London Toronto Sydney New Delhi

LITTLE SIMON

An imprint of Simon & Schuster Children's Publishing Division

1230 Avenue of the Americas, New York, New York 10020

First Little Simon paperback edition January 2023. Copyright © 2023 by Simon & Schuster, Inc. All rights reserved, including the right of reproduction in whole or in part in any form. LITTLE SIMON is a registered trademark of Simon & Schuster, Inc., and associated colophon is a trademark of Simon & Schuster, Inc. For information about special discounts for bulk purchases, please contact Simon & Schuster Special Sales at 1-866-506-1949 or business@simonandschuster.com.

The Simon & Schuster Speakers Bureau can bring authors to your live event. For more information or to book an event contact the Simon & Schuster Speakers Bureau at 1-866-248-3049 or visit our website at www.simonspeakers.com.

Designed by Laura Roode. The text of this book was set in Banda.

Manufactured in the United States of America 1222 LAK 10 9 8 7 6 5 4 3 2 1

Library of Congress Cataloging-in-Publication Data

Names: Mews, Melody, author. | Stubbings, Ellen, illustrator. Title: Mystery at Mermaid Cove / by Melody Mews ; illustrated by Ellen Stubbings. Description: First Little Simon paperback edition. | New York : Little Simon, 2023. | Series: Itty bitty Princess Kitty ; 12 | Audience: Ages 5-9. | Summary: Itty must figure out why the mermaids of Lollyland have stopped singing. Identifiers: LCCN 2022028127 (print) | LCCN 2022028128 (ebook) | ISBN 9781665928045 (paperback) | ISBN 9781665928052 (hardcover) | ISBN 9781665928069 (ebook) Subjects: CYAC: Mermaids—Fiction. | Singing—Fiction. | Cats—Fiction. | Princesses—Fiction. Classification: LCC PZ7.1.M4976 My 2023 (print) | LCC PZ7.1.M4976 (ebook) | DDC [Fic]—dc23

LC record available at https://lccn.loc.gov/2022028127

LC ebook record available at https://lccn.loc.gov/2022028128

Contents

Chapter 1   Wake-Up Call   1

Chapter 2   What Time Is It?   13

Chapter 3   View from a Cloud   25

Chapter 4   Itty Meets a Mermaid   37

Chapter 5   A Plan with Aria   49

Chapter 6   Time to Give Up?   61

Chapter 7   A Voice in the Distance   71

Chapter 8   Sunset Swim   79

Chapter 9   Mermaid Mystery: Solved!   89

Chapter 10   A Special Concert   103

Wake-Up Call

Itty Bitty Princess Kitty was fast asleep when something woke her up. She sat up in bed. It was still dark in her room. What had awakened her?

Itty was just about to snuggle back under the covers when she heard a sound. And not just any sound. It was the mermaids from Mermaid Cove singing the time. As Itty listened, the mermaids sang eight notes, which meant it was eight o'clock. It also meant she had overslept!

Itty sprang from bed. She had to get ready for school quickly! She couldn't believe she had slept so late. Her parents, the King and Queen of Lollyland, must have too, or surely one of them would have knocked on her door.

Itty was grabbing her backpack when she heard the mermaids again. This time Itty heard *six* notes, which didn't make any sense. How could it be eight o'clock and then, minutes later, six o'clock? Itty peered out the window and saw that it was still dark outside. It wasn't usually dark when she left for school.

"Itty, slow down," Queen Kitty murmured sleepily as Itty sped through the royal foyer.

"But, Mom, I'm going to be late for school!"

"Late?" The Queen looked confused. "Darling, you don't have to leave for another hour. Why are you up so early?"

Now Itty looked confused.

"I heard the mermaids singing eight notes before!"

Itty's mom smiled as she sipped her tea. "Your dad isn't even awake yet. You must have miscounted."

Itty frowned. Had she really just heard the notes wrong? Then she shrugged. "Well, I guess that means I have plenty of time for breakfast."

But by the afternoon, Itty was convinced she had not miscounted that morning. All day long, the mermaids had sung the wrong number of notes. At first Itty wondered why no one else seemed to notice.

But she realized that most of her classmates were just paying attention to their rainbow desks, which changed color when it was time for a new lesson.

Itty had always enjoyed listening to the mermaids sing the time, though. And now, Itty was sure something wasn't right with the mermaids *or* their singing.

What Time
Is It?

That evening Itty sat in the royal dining room with her father.

"Where's Mom?" Itty asked.

"I don't know. It's not like her to be late for dinner," the King replied.

Itty looked around.

Just then the Queen rushed in. She explained that she had lost track of time.

"Oh, but you haven't started," she noticed. "Where *is* dinner?" she asked as she settled into her chair.

"We haven't seen Garbanzo," Itty replied. "I can go in the kitchen and—"

Itty stopped herself. She remembered that she and her dad weren't allowed in the kitchen while the cooking fairies were working because they sometimes got in the way. Especially when they tried to sneak tastes of what the fairies were making.

"I'll go," the Queen said.

A few minutes later she returned.

"We have a problem," she announced. "Garbanzo didn't know what time it was, so dinner isn't ready. Between that, the fact that I almost missed dinner entirely, and Itty waking up early this morning, it seems like no one knows what time it is. Which means—"

"Something's going on with the mermaids," Itty finished. "I knew it. Can I go talk to them? You know how much I love their singing! And I have a good ear for music."

"That's true," the King agreed.
"She always knows when you're
off-key," he said to the Queen.

The Queen gave Itty's dad
a look. Then she turned to Itty.

"It can be difficult to befriend a mermaid," she said seriously.

"Oh yes," the King agreed. "I always make sure to bring some of Garbanzo's sugarplum candies if I have to talk to them."

The Queen continued. "Itty, there are rules to follow if you are going to meet the mermaids. It's

a big responsibility." The Queen looked thoughtful. "Of course, you handled your responsibilities at the Frost Festival perfectly. . . ."

"I can do this!" Itty promised.
Her parents exchanged smiles.
"Okay, Itty," the Queen said.
"But remember, Lollyland will be
counting on you!"

chapter 3

View from
a Cloud

"Let the mermaid approach me first," Itty recited to herself. "Compliment their singing. Present them with a gift."

It was the next morning, and Itty was ready to visit Mermaid Cove. The night before, she had memorized the rules the Queen had told her to follow. Itty peeked into her backpack to make sure she had everything.

"Snacks for later, check. Map of Mermaid Cove, check." She reached inside her backpack and touched a velvet box. "Special present for the mermaid, check."

Itty walked onto her balcony to hail a cloud. One arrived quickly and she hopped aboard.

"To Mermaid Cove!"

The cloud sped off.

Itty wondered once again what time it was. Then she remembered a lesson from school: The sun rises in the east and sets in the west. The location of the sun told her it was still morning.

But what time exactly? Itty didn't know. All she knew was that it wasn't close to lunch yet, because her tummy usually started to rumble around then. And anyway, she'd just had breakfast.

As the cloud zoomed along, Itty peered down at Lollyland. Bits of conversations drifted up.

"We had to leave without you." An annoyed giraffe was giving a message to a messenger fairy.

"I didn't know the time!" a dog said as his boss scolded him for being late to work.

Then something caught Itty's eye. Several of the homes below had large objects on their lawns. Itty realized they were sundials. Some of the residents of Lollyland were relying on sundials to know what time it was!

Suddenly the sky grew dark. Moments later, raindrops began to fall. Itty wished she had an umbrella . . . but she realized the animals on the ground had bigger problems. Their sundials wouldn't work if clouds were covering up the sun. Itty had to figure out what was going on at Mermaid Cove *now*.

Itty Meets a Mermaid

The rain stopped as quickly as it started, and before long Itty's cloud parked on the shore of Mermaid Cove.

"Thanks," Itty called as she hopped off.

Now, she had things to do!

She pulled the map out of her
backpack, looking for the dock
her parents had told her about.
She followed the map around the
cove, until finally . . .

There it is! Itty thought. She rushed ahead and climbed into the royal canoe. Everyone knew cats didn't exactly *love* the water. But what they didn't know was that the royal canoe had special powers that ensured it wouldn't tip or sink! So Itty never had to touch the water!

Itty had visited Mermaid Cove plenty of times, but this was the first time she had ever explored it by canoe.

The sun shimmered on the sea, which was calm and smooth. All was quiet, except for the gentle sound of Itty's paddling and the distant hum of a waterfall.

But suddenly Itty's ears twitched as she heard a splash. Up ahead the water rippled. And a tail appeared, and then disappeared under the surface.

A *mermaid*, Itty thought. She stopped paddling and waited.

A few moments later a mermaid emerged. She perched atop a nearby rock, basking in the sun, her back to Itty. She began to sing. Itty was mesmerized and almost paddled over to her, but then she remembered the rules her mom had told her. So she waited.

The mermaid turned so she was facing Itty. She had long, beautiful, turquoise hair and a shimmering blue tail. She smiled and waved for Itty to come forward.

Itty paddled slowly until she was close enough to the mermaid to give her the gift she had brought.

"I made this for you," Itty said shyly as she handed over the velvet box.

The mermaid took the box and slowly opened it. She gasped. "I love it!" she exclaimed as she fastened the delicate aquamarine necklace around her neck. "Now, how can I help you, Princess Itty?"

chapter 5

A Plan
with Aria

"You know who I am?" Itty asked.

"Of course." The mermaid smiled. "My name is Aria."

Itty sometimes forgot that *most* of the creatures of Lollyland knew who she was. She was the Princess, after all.

"It's nice to meet you," Itty said to Aria. "I was wondering . . . I mean, we're all wondering . . ." Itty paused. She didn't want to offend the mermaid. But she didn't know how else to say it. "What's up with your singing?" she finally blurted out.

"We've been wondering the same thing!" Aria replied.

Itty's eyes went wide.

"We're not the ones singing all those extra notes," Aria continued. "We can hear them, but none of the mermaids know who is actually singing them."

Well, *this* was a surprise!

"Some of the older mermaids are getting really annoyed," Aria added.

Itty giggled. "I think the grown-ups in Lollyland are pretty annoyed too." She told Aria about what she had heard on her trip over.

"I wish we could help, but we don't know what to do." Aria shrugged. "But thank you for visiting."

Was Aria about to dive back into the water?

"Wait!" Itty cried. She couldn't go home without solving this mystery, and she needed Aria's help. "Please, don't go," she said. "What if we explore the cove together and try to figure out who's singing those extra notes?"

Aria shook her head. "The mermaids have already searched everywhere. It's no use."

Itty had an idea. "The mermaids have probably searched everywhere in the *water*," she said. "But what if I stay above the water? That way I can see more of the cove while you continue to search. And if you sing in each place we go, I can try to listen for any extra notes."

Aria thought about this for a moment. Then she smiled. "That could work," she said slowly. "All right, I'm in!"

Time to Give Up?

Itty and Aria were just about to begin exploring when Itty's tummy rumbled.

"It's lunchtime," Itty announced, reaching into her backpack for a snack.

"How can you tell if we're not

singing the proper notes?" Aria wondered.

Itty smiled. "My *stomach* can tell." She took out her crackers. "Would you like some?" she asked Aria.

Aria yelped. "Are you eating baby *fish*?"

Itty looked down at her snack. "Oh no!" she said. "These are just crackers! They're yummy! Try some!"

"Oh . . . that's okay." Aria laughed. "Sorry, that was silly of me. It's just . . . mermaids are friends with fish."

After Itty finished her snack, they set off. Aria swam ahead to a narrow section of the cove. Itty paddled over and watched and listened carefully as Aria sang one, two, three notes.

They waited.

Moments later they heard three more notes.

Itty looked around, but they were alone.

"Could it be an echo?" Itty wondered.

Aria shook her head. "We thought about that too, but we've never had echoes here before. And besides, sometimes the number of notes that we hear back is different. And sometimes it happens when none of the mermaids have even sung one note."

"Let's keep trying," Itty said.

For a while, Itty and Aria kept exploring. Aria sang in practically every corner of the cove. She sang in shallow water and deep water. She sang perched among the coral and perched on a rock.

Each time, she would sing just one note, and each time, Itty would hear more notes moments later.

But Itty never spotted anyone else.

Finally, Itty and Aria headed back toward the shore.

"It's getting late, Princess Itty," said Aria.

Itty, too, had noticed that the sun was beginning to set. Soon it would be evening.

She didn't know the actual time . . . but was it *time* to give up?

chapter 7

A Voice
in the Distance

Itty got out of her canoe and walked slowly along the beach. She felt disappointed that she hadn't been able to solve the mystery at Mermaid Cove.

"Are you okay?" Aria asked.

"I wish we could have figured

out what was happening and fixed it," Itty replied.

Aria nodded sympathetically. "Me too. But you tried really hard, and that counts for something."

Itty smiled. She knew Aria was right, but she still felt a little sad.

"I know what will cheer you up," Aria said. "Why don't you collect some seashells to take home with you? That way, you can always remember our day together."

"Good idea!" Itty said brightly.

"The prettiest shells are at the far end of the beach." Aria pointed ahead. "If you want to go look there, I can stay here and keep an ear out for any unusual noises."

Itty dashed off. Soon she had reached the end of the beach.

As she began collecting shells,
Itty heard the faint sounds of Aria
singing in the distance.

And then something amazing happened: Itty heard someone singing along with Aria, only this other voice was much closer to her. So close that Itty could hear the slight differences in that voice and the mermaid's voice. The voice close to her was singing on key, but their voice was *much* deeper than a mermaid's. In fact, the more Itty listened, the more she had a feeling that the voice didn't belong to a mermaid at all!

Sunset
Swim

Itty crept slowly toward a dark
grotto up ahead. It sounded like
the voice was coming from there.

Just then, Aria's song ended, but
the mystery singer kept singing.

"Aria!" Itty cried, racing back
to the mermaid. "I think I found

our mystery singer! They're in a grotto at the end of the beach. I'm going to go search." She hopped back into her canoe.

Aria looked nervous. "Do you think that's a good idea? Won't it be dark soon?"

Aria was right; it *would* be dark soon. But when? Itty didn't know—and neither would the animals of Lollyland if they didn't get the time-telling back on track.

"I'm going," Itty said. "Lollyland is counting on me!"

"Well then, I'm coming too!" Aria replied.

So they set off—Itty in her canoe and Aria swimming alongside. The sun was starting to set over the water. Suddenly, Itty heard Aria cry out!

"Help! Sea monster!"

Itty almost jumped overboard to help Aria. But then she remembered the whole water thing. She noticed some glowfish swimming by.

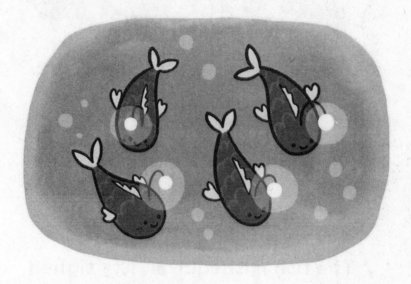

"A mermaid needs help!" she called out. "Can you light things up over here?"

The fish rushed over. Itty sighed with relief as she realized there was no sea monster—just lots of seaweed.

Aria stopped struggling and quickly freed herself. "Thanks for having those glowfish shed light on things," she joked.

Soon, Itty and Aria reached the entrance to the grotto.

"It's *really* dark in there," Itty whispered.

"We don't have to go in," Aria responded, her voice a little shaky.

Itty took a deep breath. She listened to the beautiful singing coming from inside the grotto. So much like a mermaid's . . . but also so different.

She *had* to know who it was.

Mermaid Mystery: Solved!

Itty and Aria entered the dark grotto. The mystery singer's voice was louder and clearer than ever.

"Whoever this is, they have a beautiful voice," Aria said.

Itty agreed.

As they rounded a bend, Itty

saw light up ahead. A large group of fireflies was hovering in the air, providing enough light that it was no longer too dark to see.

"I think they like the singing too," Aria murmured.

Just then, the singing stopped. "Who—who's there?" someone asked.

"I'm Princess Itty," Itty called out. "I'm here with my friend Aria. We'd like to talk to you."

A few moments passed and then a large creature moved toward them. It was swimming, but its head was above water. Itty and Aria both backed up as it approached. Finally, when the creature appeared, Itty realized it was a narwhal!

"Hi!" said the narwhal. "My name is Nate."

"I've never met a narwhal before!" Itty exclaimed.

"Me neither," said Aria.

"Well, I've never met a princess or a mermaid!" Nate replied, and everyone laughed.

"You said you wanted to talk to me," Nate said.

Itty explained to Nate what was happening in Lollyland.

"I had no idea anyone could hear my singing," Nate said. "I'm so sorry. I'll never sing again!"

"You don't have to stop singing," Itty said quickly. "Your voice is wonderful. But it *has* been causing some problems when it gets mixed up with the mermaids.'"

"You think my voice is wonderful?" Nate asked.

Itty and Aria both nodded enthusiastically.

Even the fireflies flickered in agreement.

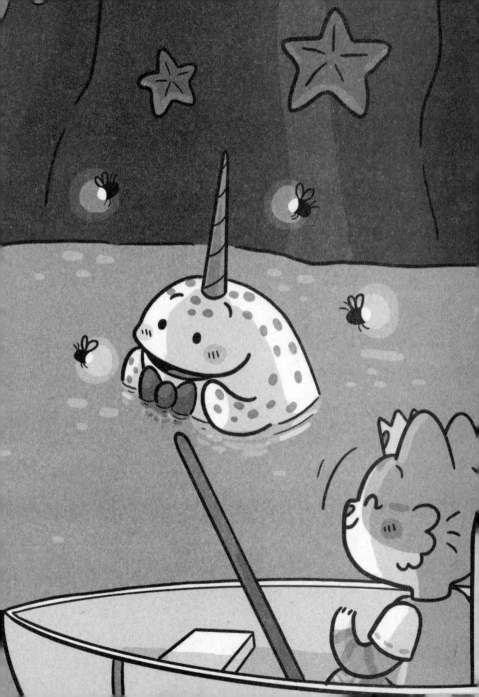

"I can't believe a mermaid and a princess think my singing is good!" cried Nate. A proud smile spread over his face. "You see, I hide in here because I thought no one would want to hear me. Narwhals aren't exactly known for their singing."

Itty thought about this. And then she had an idea—an idea about how to fix the time-telling problems  in Lollyland *and* give Nate an opportunity to show off his beautiful voice.

A Special
Concert

It was a few weeks later. Itty and her friends Luna Unicorn, Esme Butterfly, and Chipper Bunny had just been dropped off at Mermaid Cove. Itty had a surprise for them.

Right after Itty and Aria had discovered Nate, things had returned to normal in Lollyland. Once again, the mermaids were singing the correct number of notes, which meant the creatures of Lollyland always knew what time it was. But now it wasn't *just* the mermaids who were singing the time. Nate was singing with them!

"So what's our surprise?" Esme asked as she fluttered ahead.

"You'll find out soon enough," Itty responded.

"Give me a hint," Luna pleaded. "You know how I am with surprises!" Glitter was already spouting from her horn, which happened when she got excited.

"She's got a point there," Chipper added.

"Okay, I'll tell you now, but just so you can get the glitter part over with," Itty said.

Then she told her friends about the special concert they were about to attend.

"Oh my!" Luna cried, glitter flying everywhere. "Mermaids *and* a narwhal?"

"Will there be snacks?" Chipper asked.

"Definitely," Itty assured him. "Just no fish-shaped crackers. I'll explain later. Okay, it's time!"

They sat down on the shore. Suddenly, Nate popped out of the water and waved to Itty and her friends.

And then slowly, one by one, seven mermaids popped up and formed a circle around Nate.

They began to sing. Nate harmonized perfectly with the mermaids.

"This is *amazing*," Luna whispered excitedly. "I had no idea narwhals could sing like that!"

"Neither did Nate." Itty giggled. "But thanks to the Lollyland mermaids, now he believes in himself."

"*And* thanks to you," Luna whispered back.

Itty grinned. It felt good to have helped Nate and to have solved the mystery at Mermaid Cove. Plus, Lollyland was finally back on schedule. Though Itty wondered now if she should have asked the mermaids to push back the morning wake-up call by a few minutes. *Oh well*, she thought. And with that, she smiled to herself and enjoyed the show.

Itty has lots of stories to share!

If you like Itty's adventures, then you'll love . . .

the CRitteR club

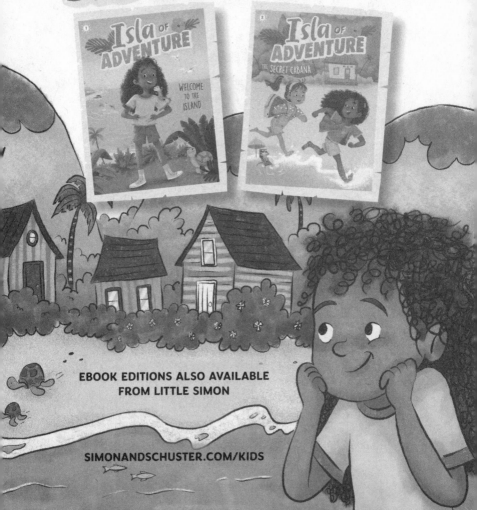

the adventures of
SOPHIE MOUSE